Pig Pig
Goes to Camp

by David McPhail

E. P. DUTTON · NEW YORK

Copyright © 1983 by David McPhail

Library of Congress Cataloging in Publication Data
McPhail, David.
   Pig pig goes to camp.
   Summary: Pig Pig finally agrees to go to camp
for the summer and has a wonderful time.
   [1. Pigs—Fiction.   2. Camping—Fiction]
I. Title.
PZ7.M4789Pi   1983   [E]   83-1412
ISBN 0-525-44064-X

Published in the United States by E. P. Dutton, Inc.,
2 Park Avenue, New York, N.Y. 10016
Published simultaneously in Canada by Clarke,
Irwin & Company Limited, Toronto and Vancouver
Editor: Ann Durell   Designer: Riki Levinson
Printed in Hong Kong by South China Printing Co.
First Edition
10 9 8 7 6 5 4 3 2 1

Every summer Pig Pig's mother
asked him if he wanted to go to camp.
And Pig Pig always said "NO!"

But after he grew up, Pig Pig changed his mind.
"Can I go to camp this summer?" he
asked his mother.
"Of course, dear," answered his mother.

So Pig Pig prepared to go to camp.
He packed his toothbrush and tail comb,
some postcards, stamps, his bathing suit
and plenty of clean underwear.

The next morning, Pig Pig kissed
his mother good-bye and boarded the
bus to Camp Wildhog.

When he arrived at camp, Pig Pig
was assigned to tent number 7, along
with three other young pigs.

Pig Pig really enjoyed camp.

The woods were wonderful—most of the time.

The lake was perfect

for diving

and swimming...

and boating.

Pig Pig even learned water safety and first aid.

Pig Pig participated in sports...

and during crafts he braided a belt
of green and purple plastic.

He learned to cook over a campfire.

Pig Pig wrote to his mother once a week.
He told her he liked everyone at camp…

especially the cook.

But what Pig Pig loved most at camp
were the frogs. They were everywhere!

There were frogs in the lake,

frogs in the trees,

frogs in the grass...

and even
frogs in the sleeping bags!

Almost everyone at camp hated those
frogs. But not Pig Pig. He loved them,
and they loved him!

When Pig Pig went swimming,
the frogs went swimming.

When Pig Pig went boating,
the frogs went boating.

When Pig Pig sat down to supper,
the frogs were all over him,
and all over the table.

But Pig Pig didn't mind.
He didn't even mind that at night
there was hardly any room in his sleeping
bag for *him*, it was so full of frogs.

Pig Pig was happy. Everyone else
was miserable.

The camp director decided to take
action. He wrote to Pig Pig's mother.

"We are sending Pig Pig home," the letter read. "He has enjoyed himself very much, and his conduct has been excellent. He has simply become too popular.

Signed:

The Camp Director

P.S. He is bringing home some of his friends."

Just then Pig Pig's bus pulled up, and
Pig Pig's mother went outside to meet him.